Cinderella

A Tale of Kindness

Retold by Sarah Price
Illustrated by Mary Hanson-Roberts

Famous Fables

Reader's Digest Young Families

Once upon a time, a beautiful young girl lived with her stepmother and two stepsisters. While the girl was kind and sweet-natured, her stepmother and stepsisters were vain and not nice at all. All day the girl had to cook and clean. She never complained.

Every night after the girl finished her chores, she would sit by the chimney among the cinders and ashes to warm her cold, tired feet. And that is why she was called Cinderella.

One day, the king announced there would be a ball for two nights. Everyone in the kingdom was invited.

"Cinderella, wouldn't you like to go to the ball?" asked the older stepsister, smiling meanly.

"Oh, yes," answered Cinderella with a sigh. "But how could I go when I have nothing to wear?"

"You are right," replied the younger stepsister. "Everyone would laugh to see you in your rags!"

On the eve of the ball, Cinderella watched her family ride away. She was very sad.

Suddenly Cinderella's fairy godmother appeared. "What is it that you wish for, my dear?" she asked.

"I wish I could go to the ball," said Cinderella.

Cinderella's godmother smiled. "Well, then you shall go, my dear. Run into the garden and bring me back a pumpkin and two animal traps."

Cinderella did as she was told. The fairy raised her wand and tapped the pumpkin. It instantly became a fine carriage.

Next, the godmother told Cinderella to open the traps. The fairy tapped each animal with her wand as it ran out. The mice became six handsome horses. The rats became two fat coachmen. The lizards made four handsome footmen.

The godmother smiled at Cinderella. "There you are, my dear. Will this do?"

"Oh, yes!" cried Cinderella. Then she looked down at her tattered gray dress. "But I have nothing to wear."

Her godmother touched her with her wand. Instantly, Cinderella's rags turned into a shimmering gown. Glittering jewels adorned her hair and neck. Sparkling glass slippers appeared on her little feet.

"Now off you go," her godmother said. "But listen well—you must leave the ball before the clock strikes midnight! At exactly twelve o'clock, your carriage will change back to a pumpkin, your horses to mice, your coachmen to rats, and your footmen to lizards. And your clothes will be as they were before."

"Yes, I promise," said Cinderella excitedly.

When Cinderella entered the ballroom, everyone gazed in wonder. The girl looked like a princess, but no one knew who she was.

The prince gave Cinderella his hand and led her to the dance floor. He danced with her all evening. At fifteen minutes before midnight, Cinderella curtsied to the prince and hurried away.

As soon as Cinderella arrived home, she thanked her godmother with all her heart. Her stepmother and stepsisters returned not long afterward.

"Did you have a good time?" asked Cinderella.

"No," said the older stepsister. "A princess was there who danced with the prince the whole time."

"But," added the younger one, "she was kind and beautiful, and she graciously spoke with us."

The next night, Cinderella arrived at the ball
dressed even more beautifully than before. The prince
remained by her side all evening. She was having such
a wonderful time, she forgot all about her promise to her
godmother. Then she heard the clock striking midnight!

Cinderella ran out of the hall. The prince raced
after her, desperate to know her name, but she
disappeared. In her haste, Cinderella left one glass
slipper on the steps. The prince picked it up carefully.

Cinderella ran all the way home. Her elegant
clothes were gone, except for one glass slipper.

The prince proclaimed that he would marry the maiden whose foot fit the slipper. The prince's footmen traveled through the kingdom, trying the slipper on all the young ladies.

At last, the glass slipper was brought to Cinderella's home. Each stepsister tried to force her foot into the little shoe, but the slipper was far too small.

Then Cinderella asked, "May I try on the slipper?"

Her stepsisters burst out laughing at such an idea, but the footman looked closely at Cinderella. He could see that she was very beautiful. He declared that he had orders to let every maiden try on the slipper.

The glass slipper fit Cinderella's foot perfectly! Cinderella pulled the other slipper out of her pocket and put it on. Her stepmother and stepsisters nearly fainted with astonishment.

Cinderella's fairy godmother appeared at that moment and touched her wand to Cinderella's clothes. Instantly the rags changed into a beautiful gown.

Only then did Cinderella's stepmother and stepsisters recognize her as the mysterious princess. They fell to their knees and begged her forgiveness for how poorly they had treated her. Cinderella pulled them to their feet and embraced them.

The footmen took Cinderella to the palace. The prince was overcome with joy to see her again. On bended knee, he asked her to marry him, and she happily accepted. Cinderella and the prince were married the very next day.

Cinderella, who was as kind as she was beautiful, arranged for her stepmother and stepsisters to live at the palace. She even introduced her stepsisters to two noblemen whom they married, and they all lived happily ever after.

Famous Fables, Lasting Virtues
Tips for Parents

Now that you've read Cinderella, *use these pages as a guide in teaching your child the virtues in the story. By talking about the story and its message and engaging in the suggested activities, you can help your child develop good judgment and a strong moral character.*

About Kindness

Young children have a natural sense of empathy toward others. The challenge for parents is to encourage and nurture this tendency, so that their youngsters grow up to be kind and empathic people. How can you strengthen your child's natural inclination to be kind?

1. *Be a role model.* If you show kindness toward others, your child will learn to do the same. Smile at people you encounter in the course of your day. Thank the salesperson at the store. Help elderly people who are loading groceries into their cars. As is so often true when instilling values in children, actions speak louder than words.

2. *Teach your children to be kind to others.* Praise every act of kindness, even the smallest ones, performed by your child. Gently guide your little one's good behavior by encouraging her to eat lunch with a new child at school and to share her toys with playmates. If your child does something thoughtless or unkind, tell her that the behavior is unacceptable. Focus on the act, rather than on the child ("Your behavior was not kind." versus "You are not very nice.").

3. *Evaluate your child's books and videos.* Limit your child's time with books, videos, and TV programs that show violence or that glamorize characters who act dishonorably. Studies have shown that children who watch too much violence behave with less empathy toward others. Instead, look for books and videos that show kids helping others.